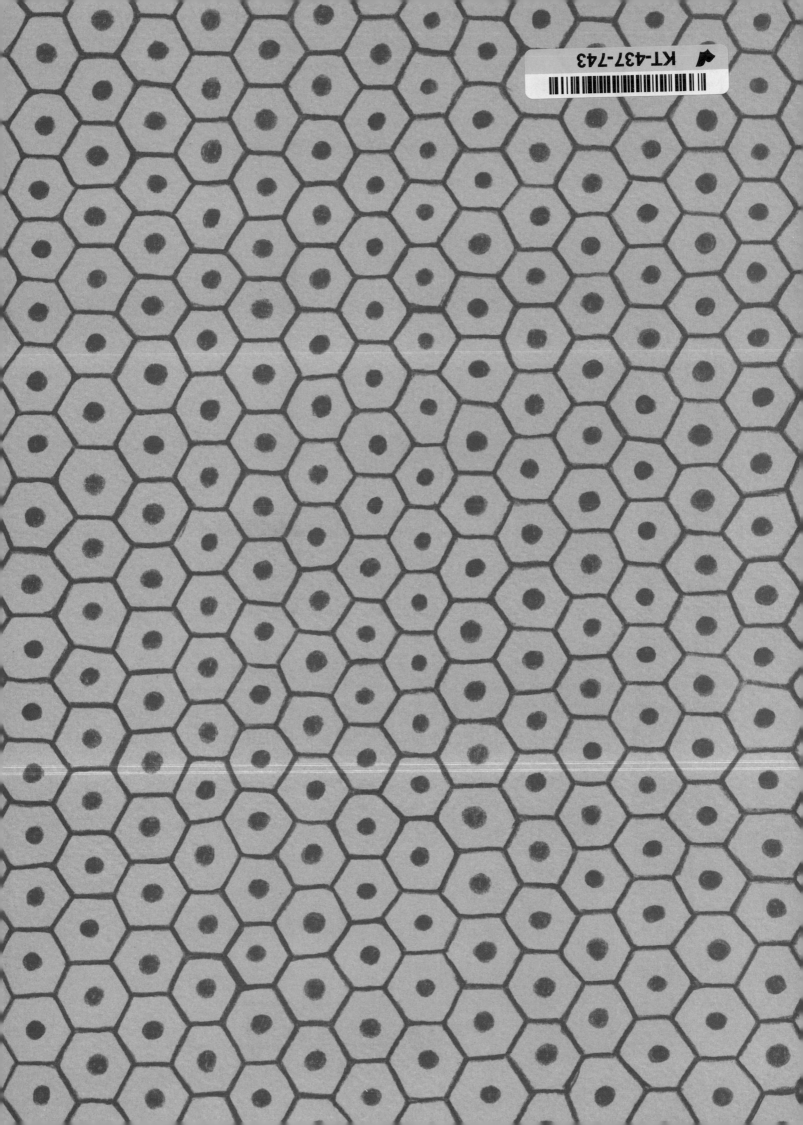

Published by
Princeton Architectural Press
A McEvoy Group company
202 Warren Street
Hudson, New York 12534
Visit our website at www.papress.com

First published in France under the title: *Au lit Miyuki*
© 2017, De La Martinière Jeunesse, a division of La Martinière Groupe, Paris

Princeton Architectural Press is a leading publisher in architecture, design,
photography, landscape, and visual culture. We create fine books and stationery
of unsurpassed quality and production values. With more than one thousand
titles published, we find design everywhere and in the most unlikely places.

This book was illustrated using watercolors and colored pencils.

Editors: Amy Novesky and Nina Pick
Typesetting: Paul Wagner

Special thanks to: Ryan Alcazar, Janet Behning, Nolan Boomer, Abby Bussel,
Benjamin English, Jan Cigliano Hartman, Susan Hershberg, Kristen Hewitt,
Lia Hunt, Valerie Kamen, Jennifer Lippert, Sara McKay, Eliana Miller, Wes Seeley,
Sara Stemen, Marisa Tesoro, and Joseph Weston of Princeton Architectural Press
—Kevin C. Lippert, publisher

Library of Congress Cataloging-in-Publication Data
Names: Galliez, Roxane Marie, author. | Ratanavanh, Seng Soun, 1974-
    illustrator.
Title: Time for bed, Miyuki / Roxane Marie Galliez ; illustrated by Seng Soun
    Ratanavanh.
Other titles: Au lit Miyuki. English
Description: English edition. | New York : Princeton Architectural Press,
    [2018]. | "First published in France under the title: Au lit Miyuki
    2017"—Title page verso. | Summary: When Grandfather calls Miyuki to bed,
    she persuades him to help prepare for a visit from the Dragonfly Queen,
    cover the cat, and more before she is finally ready to sleep.
Identifiers: LCCN 2017037150 | ISBN 9781616897055 (alk. paper)
Subjects: | CYAC: Bedtime—Fiction. | Grandfathers—Fiction. |
    Nature—Fiction.
Classification: LCC PZ7.G1373 Tim 2018 | DDC [E]—dc23
LC record available at https://lccn.loc.gov/2017037150

TEXT BY

Roxane Marie Galliez

ILLUSTRATIONS BY

Seng Soun Ratanavanh

Time for Bed, Miyuki

PRINCETON ARCHITECTURAL PRESS

NEW YORK

With a rain of gold on silver hills, the sun offers its
last light before leaving for the night. The nightingale
prepares her nest. Ants gather their provisions.
And the toad jumps into a bucket. As the sun slowly
hides to watch the moon rise, the bell tower sounds
the hour of rest.

But where is Miyuki?

Miyuki is busy playing and trying to push back time.
Grandfather is trying to get her to go to bed.

"Miyuki, it's time for bed."
"Not yet, Grandfather. Look, the sun hasn't set yet,
and I still have so much to do."
"What do you have to do that cannot wait until
tomorrow, Miyuki?"

"Why, I must prepare for the arrival of the Dragonfly Queen," Miyuki said. "She chose our garden to visit tomorrow, and she will bring her entire court."

"Her entire court?" Grandfather asked.

"Yes, it's a very big deal. Can you please help me make a canopy to honor her, there, under the cherry tree?" Miyuki asked politely.

"All right, my Miyuki, and then it's time for bed."

So Grandfather helped Miyuki make a canopy fit for a queen with fallen leaves, three twigs, and a poppy.

"Miyuki, it's time for bed."

"But Grandfather, I must water my vegetables."

"All right, Miyuki," Grandfather sighed.

"Water your vegetables, and then it's time for bed."

Miyuki watered her carrots, turnips, radishes,
and everything else she could reach. How many
times did Miyuki go from the well to the garden?
Even Grandfather stopped counting.

"Miyuki, the canopy for the Queen is complete
and your vegetable garden is watered. It's time for bed."
"Grandfather, I cannot sleep now!" Miyuki cried.
"I must gather the whole Snail family together. If they
are not gathered together, I will not be able to sleep."

So Grandfather helped Miyuki look for the snails
and lead them all home.

"Miyuki, the canopy for the Queen is complete,
your vegetable garden is watered, the snails
are gathered. It's time for bed."

"But Grandfather, I can't stop now. It's a cold night,
and I won't be able to fall asleep if I haven't covered
up the cat."

Patiently, Grandfather waited as Miyuki covered
their cat with a warm blanket.

"Miyuki, the canopy for the Queen is complete,
your vegetable garden is watered, the snails
are gathered, the cat is covered. It's time for bed."
"Oh, Grandfather, we must dance the last dance
of the day, to thank the sun for shining so nicely."

So Grandfather and Miyuki danced.

And then, Miyuki yawned...

"Miyuki, the canopy for the Queen is complete,
your vegetable garden is watered, the snails are gathered,
the cat is covered, and we danced the last dance of
the day. It's time for bed," Grandfather said wearily.

Miyuki's eyes were growing heavy. But there was
still work to be done.

"Grandfather, I cannot go to bed until I've bathed and
brushed my hair. And what will the stars say if
I am not in my best pajamas when they visit me?"

So Grandfather prepared Miyuki's bath, brushed her
hair, and laid out her best pajamas for her to wear.

Then, Miyuki yawned again.
And Grandfather yawned too.

"Miyuki, the canopy for the Queen is complete,
your vegetable garden is watered, the snails are gathered,
the cat is covered, we danced the last dance of the day,
you're bathed and brushed and dressed. It's time for bed."

This time Miyuki didn't argue. She took Grandfather's
hand and followed him. Grandfather tucked Miyuki
into bed and kissed her on the forehead.

"Grandfather," she whispered.
"We forgot to do something very important…"
"I know, Miyuki, I have not forgotten.
I will tell you a story."

Grandfather opened a book and began to read.

With a rain of gold on silver hills, the sun
offers its last light before leaving for the night.
The nightingale prepares her nest. Ants gather
their provisions. And the toad jumps into
a bucket. As the sun slowly hides to watch the
moon rise, the bell tower sounds the hour of rest.

But where is Miyuki?

Shh…

I think Miyuki has fallen asleep.

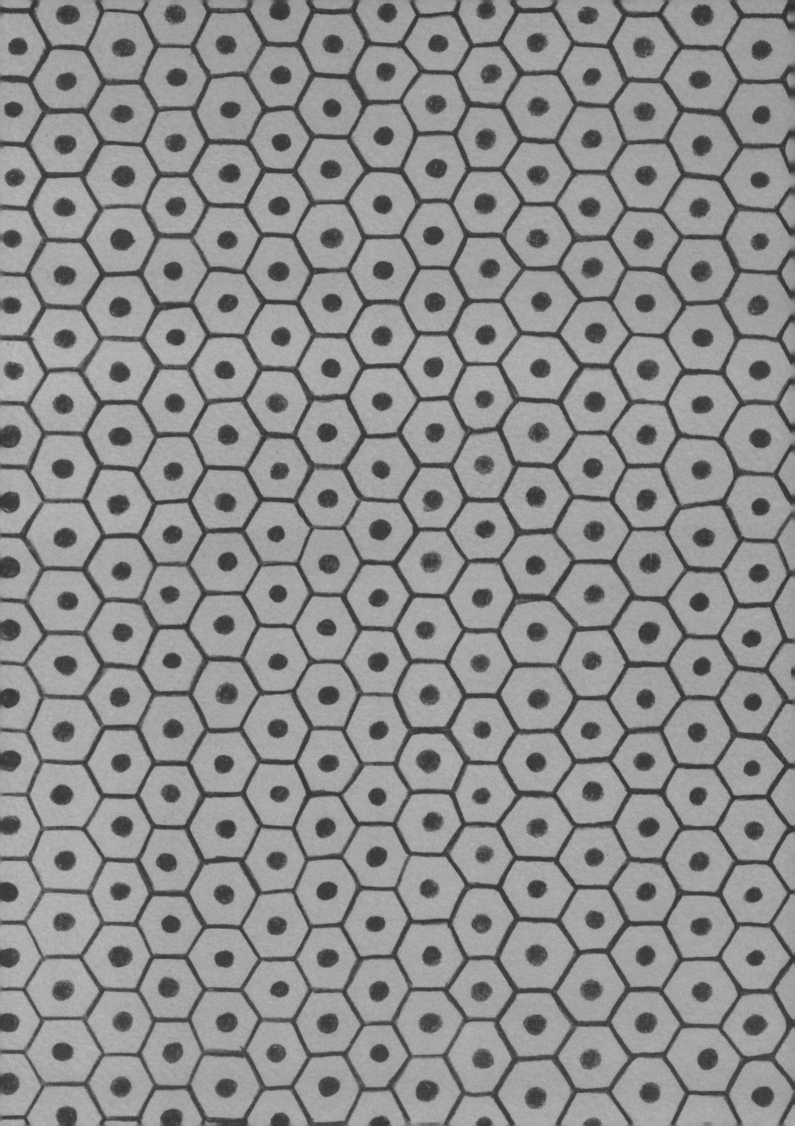